Boy Without a Home

DEBBIE VIALE

Copyright © 2022 by Debbie Viale

Hardcover: 978-1-958381-27-4
Paperback: 978-1-958381-03-8
eBook: 978-1-958381-02-1
Library of Congress Control Number: 2022910093

This is a work of fiction.

Once upon a time

There was a boy that had no home

He roamed the streets all alone

One day he came across an owl and
asked him if he had some chow

Now the owl didn't care too much
for kids so he flapped his wings
And shouted Hoo! Hoo! Hoo!

So the boy ran off in a state of shock

12
1
2
3
4
5
6
7
8
9
10
11

Then he stopped in front
of a great big clock

He asked the clock to
give him the time

Tik! Tok! Tik! Tok!

But the clock just muttered,
tick tock tick tock

So off he went until he
found a tiny little mouse

Outside a tiny little house

The boy asked the mouse who
was eating a chunk of cheese

Can you spare a nibble
for me please?

So the mouse climbed
up and rang the bell

When an old man opened
the door and said

Come on in and sit for a spell

I have a fire, I have a wife.
She cooks all day and
cleans til night

But all of our children, went away

So come inside.
We hope you'll stay

34

We have lots of toys and lots of food

And apple pie that's really good

Author: Debbie Viale'

I grew up in a small town by the San Francisco Bay "Martinez" Ca. I started writing at age 14 and published many poems through the years. I'm living on a Horse Ranch now and use a lot of my short stories to entertain my 5 grandchildren. So I decided to publish several stories they enjoy.

Illustrator: Erin Benzler

I live in Antioch Ca. And I grew an interest with art at a young age due to my Dad who was an artist. I grew up watching him and he is my inspiration.